THE SEA

DOES NOT CARE

HAKIM IBN ADAM

DEDICATION

To the process.

Contents

PRE-DAWN

Four-thirty: neither night nor morning, that temporal membrane where circadian certainty falters. His waking is not arrival but continuation—consciousness emerging from metabolic slowness into a darkness, which is not the Northern cities' darkness.

Sound announces what light withholds. The sea's breathing, arterial and venous, systolic compression and diastolic release—not metaphor but structural homology. Through closed shutters, through concrete and plaster, through the medium of air itself, the Mediterranean performs its existence without witness. The baker's motorcycle coughs to life three streets away. A cat disturbs something metallic in the alley. Alexandria's pre-dawn orchestra tunes itself according to no conductor, each instrument entering when internal necessity dictates.

He does not turn on the lights. The phosphorescent numerals of his watch—radium-226 decaying with its half-life of sixteen hundred years—provide the only visible certainty. Time measured by atomic deterioration, entropy made useful. His feet sense the floor's temperature, fourteen degrees cooler than the body's core, thermal gradients establishing themselves according to laws that precede consciousness and will outlast it. To dress in darkness is to discover clothing's phenomenology stripped of visual confirmation. The shirt was recently purchased from a shop whose proprietor spoke an Arabic accelerated beyond his dormant comprehension.

The door's lock mechanism—pin tumbler design, invented in ancient Egypt, releases with metallic certainty. The hallway's darkness differs from the apartment's: communal, traversed, carrying traces of neighbours he hasn't met.

Three floors descended, each landing a pause in gravitational negotiation. Architecture as arrested flow—the building settling into its foundations with barely perceptible adjustments, Portland cement's calcium silicates frozen mid-reaction, permanent but not eternal. The street door opens onto what he imagined as the philosophical city of Alexandria, before actual Alexandria wakes.

East. The cardinal direction chosen not by decision but by something prior to choice. The kind of knowledge the body harbours below consciousness. He walks toward where the sun will appear, but it has not yet announced itself toward where the Mediterranean curves away from Africa toward Asia, toward waters that have been wine-dark and rosy-fingered. Simply water, the accumulation of hydrogen and oxygen molecules held in a liquid state by temperature and pressure conditions specific to this planet's distance from its star.

The Corniche reveals itself through tactile and olfactory intelligence. Salt's crystalline presence, sodium chloride in aerosol suspension, deposits itself on the lips, accumulates in the nasal passages, and infiltrates the lungs with each inhalation. The sea's chemistry written in air: not just salt but sulphur compounds from algae, trace metals from three continents' erosion, hydrocarbons from yesterday's fishing boats. The smell is not memory—memory would be representation, mediation—but direct molecular encounter, olfactory receptors binding to specific compounds, electrochemical signals racing along cranial nerve one to the limbic system, where emotion and memory interweave below the threshold of language.

His feet find the sea wall's edge through proprioceptive calculation, the body's knowledge of its own position in space. Limestone blocks quarried from Tura, the same source as the pyramids, though these nineteenth-century installments lack their ancestors' precision. The stone is still warm from yesterday's solar collection, thermal mass releasing photon-gifted energy back to the cooler air. He places both palms flat against the stone, feeling its granular texture, calcium carbonate skeletons of marine organisms compressed over geological time into this solid that pretends permanence while slowly dissolving, molecule by molecule, back into the sea that made it.

The Mediterranean's sound here is not singular but multiple: waves against stone, water withdrawing over shingle, the deeper percussion of swells meeting the continental shelf. Each wave's acoustic signature is unique, unrepeatable, though the pattern persists. Frequency and amplitude encode information about wind speed, fetch distance, and seafloor topography. The sea speaks in languages older than human speech, older than vertebrate evolution, the dialogue between water and shore that began when Earth's surface cooled enough to permit liquid's existence.

Behind him, the city's electrical grid maintains its hum, alternating current flowing through copper arteries, resistance generating heat, entropy tax paid on civilization's luminous ambitions. Street lights—high-pressure sodium lamps emitting their characteristic yellow—create pools of visibility that paradoxically deepen the surrounding darkness. But he stands beyond their reach, in the liminal zone where artificial illumination surrenders to its absence.

The sea neither awaits nor anticipates, yet its waiting is its work. This thought arrives unbidden, the kind of formation that emerges from the interface between consciousness and its environment. He reaches for the notebook in his pocket—leather-bound, pages cream-colored though invisible now, purchased from the same shop as the shirt. The fountain pen's weight is familiar in fingers that have written countless reports, diagnostic assessments, where precision saves lives or confirms their conclusion. But here, in darkness, writing becomes purely kinesthetic, trust in the hand's learned patterns, muscle memory of letter formation.

Process without a witness remains process. The circulation continues whether observed or not, blood through vessels, currents through waters, thoughts through neural networks. To stand before the invisible sea is to confront epistemology's limits: what can be known without light? Everything essential. The wave-function doesn't collapse until measurement, but the waves themselves collapse continuously against this shore, measured by stone's erosion, by the salt crystallizing on my skin, by the pressure variations in my cochlea. I am not observing the sea. We are co-constituting this moment, this interface, this participation.

The pen stops. To write philosophy in darkness is to trust that patterns persist and ink's molecular bonds with cellulose will hold until photons permit their reading.

East, the horizon remains indistinguishable from the sea, darkness uniform but not undifferentiated. The eye's rods, more sensitive than cones, detect variations in what seems uniformly dark. Scotopic vision, they called it in medical school, from the Greek skotos, darkness. Twenty minutes required for rhodopsin regeneration, the eye's chemistry adapting to darkness as blood chemistry adapts to altitude, as gut bacteria adapt to diet, as the sea itself adapts to temperature, salinity, and the Nile's seasonal contributions.

A fisherman passes, invisible except for his cigarette's ember and the plastic bucket's scrape against pavement. They don't speak—what language would suffice? Arabic, which Hakim once knew but now knows he doesn't? English, which would mark him as foreign? French, Alexandria's colonial ghost language? Silence serves better, acknowledging co-presence without demanding communication. The fisherman continues west, toward the harbour, toward boats that will venture out before light, reading the sea through sonar, GPS, technologies that exceed human senses while remaining extensions of them.

The first grey. Not yet light but light's rumour, the eastern sky's density shifting, becoming less opaque. The transition is not sudden but proceeds by infinitesimal gradations, like a fever breaking, like consciousness emerging from anesthesia. The horizon begins to declare itself, a line dividing two darknesses, sea from sky, though the division is cognitive projection, atmosphere and hydrosphere interfacing without boundary, water vapour rising, condensing, precipitating, the planet's circulatory system operating at scales from molecular to global.

He remains standing, waiting without expectation, or rather with expectation stripped of specific content. The sea will become visible—this much is certain. But which sea? The Mediterranean of classical antiquity, wine-dark, Homeric, travelled by Phoenicians who invented the alphabet to track commercial transactions, an abstraction born from commerce? The Arab Sea, Bahr al-Rum, the Roman Sea that outlasted Rome? The contemporary sea, warming, acidifying, its fish populations collapsing, its waters carrying microplastics that enter food chains, that accumulate in tissues, that will outlast the civilizations that produced them?

All these seas. None of them. The sea is a process, not a product; circulation, not a container.

Before dawn, blood circulates unseen through vessels mapped but not transparent. The doctor knows without seeing: here the carotid, here the jugular, here the subclavian artery. Knowledge through palpation, through pressure, through the pulse that announces hydraulic certainty. The sea's pulse against this stone is not metaphorical correspondence but structural echo—fluid dynamics operating at different scales, same mathematics governing both flows. To feel one is to understand the other. This is not an analogy but homology.

The notebook closes. The darkness continues its slow dissolution. Alexandria stirs—a door opening, a motor starting, a child's cry from an upper window immediately hushed. The city's metabolic rate increases, ATP hydrolysis accelerating in millions of cells in thousands of bodies beginning their day's labour. Hakim turns east, toward the light that has not yet arrived but whose arrival is encoded in the planet's rotation, in the solar system's architecture, in the cosmos's expansion from its original singularity, all of history contracted into this moment of waiting for dawn over the Mediterranean, which doesn't wait but continues its processes indifferent to observation, though observation changes everything, always has.

DAWN

Grey admits colour gradually, reluctantly, as if skeptical of its own spectrum. Five-thirty and walking east along the Corniche, He moves through air that carries yesterday's heat in thermal pockets, zones where temperature varies by degrees that skin registers but consciousness barely notes. The sea to his left remains more heard than seen, though seeing has begun its uncertain establishment. Not yet the Mediterranean's notorious blue but a grey that contains blue's possibility, as RNA contains protein's possibility, as the fertilized cell contains the organism's entire future, potential waiting for conditions that permit expression.

The horizon sharpens. Where before was undifferentiated darkness, now emerges the line that philosophy has contemplated since philosophy began contemplating: the boundary that is not boundary, the division that connects what it divides. Sea meeting sky, or sky meeting sea, the prepositions revealing their inadequacy. They don't meet—they *inter-are*, to use a Buddhist formulation that participatory process monism would recognize, though recognition across traditions is always translation, always transformation, never simple equivalence.

Light's epistemology reveals itself in stages. First, the discrimination of forms: this is a building, that is a tree, there is the sea wall's edge. Then texture: the water's surface is not uniform but structured by waves, each catching dawn light differently, creating patterns that exist only in this specific angular relationship between observer, surface, and sun still below the horizon. Then colour, emerging not all at once but sequentially, as if the visible spectrum remembers its own order, red wavelengths first, seven hundred nanometers, then orange, yellow, the others waiting their turn.

A fisherman prepares his boat, the same or a different fisherman from before—in this light, individual identity remains uncertain. The boat is small, painted blue like every fishing boat on this coast, as if the sea demands chromatic harmony from those who would harvest it. The man works with practiced efficiency, movements economical, each gesture necessary, nothing wasted. This is knowledge incarnate: not theory but practice, not abstract but embodied, the kind of knowing that comes only from repetition, from participation, from submitting to the sea's teaching, which is not kind but is consistent.

The sun approaches. Not visible yet, but announced by the eastern sky's inflammation, red-orange spreading like a histological stain revealing cellular structure. The comparison arrives—eosin and hematoxylin, the dyes that make cells visible under microscopy, that reveal what light alone cannot show. Dawn is a diagnostic tool, revealing the day's potential. The sky's colour intensifies, deepens, and suddenly—though suddenly is wrong, the process being continuous—the sun's edge breaches the horizon.

The moment resists description even as it demands it. Every dawn is structurally identical—the planet's rotation bringing this longitude into solar exposure—and every dawn is unique—this cloud configuration, this atmospheric condition, this observer. Heraclitus: The sun is new every day. Literally true, the sun's fusion processes ensure that today's photons differ from yesterday's, though the pattern persists. Eight minutes and twenty seconds those photons travelled, the speed of light through vacuum being constant, to arrive at this retina, these rhodopsin molecules, this consciousness that transforms electromagnetic radiation into meaning.

The sea begins its chromatic transformation. Grey yields to silver as the angle of incidence shifts, as wavelengths segregate according to their energies. The water is not blue—water is colourless—but water in sufficient depth absorbs red wavelengths, reflects blue, creates the appearance that language solidifies into identity: the blue Mediterranean. But now, in dawn's light, it is not blue but a complexity that language fails to specify: silver-gold-grey with undertones of green where algae concentrate, purple where depth increases, white where waves break, each colour a function of physics, chemistry, biology, observation angle, and cognitive processing.

Hakim watches the sun climb, its movement imperceptible moment to moment but obvious across minutes. The Earth rotates at roughly one thousand miles per hour at this latitude, but the sensation is stillness. Motion relative to what? The question physics answers mathematically, but philosophy continues to probe.

A young woman passes, hijab bright green, smartphone

in hand, earbuds delivering private sound into her consciousness. She doesn't see him, doesn't see the sea, her attention absorbed by the screen's mediation. This, too, is Alexandria: not the ancient city of libraries and lighthouses but the contemporary city of five million, of unemployment, of young people planning emigration even as they walk along the Corniche their grandparents walked. She pauses, removes one earbud, takes a selfie with the sunrise behind her, and posts it to a platform that currently carries identity performances across networks. The image will circulate, accumulate likes, become data, contribute to algorithms that shape what others see, what becomes visible, and what remains dark.

Light enables sight but also blinds. These sunrise photographs proliferating across networks—do they document dawn or replace it? The image is more real than the experience, the documentation preceding the event it documents.

The light is changing again, gold yielding to white as the sun climbs higher. The sea's blue begins asserting itself, dozens of blues, hundreds, each wave face its own shade, the colour constantly reconstituting itself like blood cells constantly renewed, the body maintaining itself through controlled death and rebirth, apoptosis and regeneration in balance.

A coffee vendor has established operations, the

equipment minimal—gas burner, pot, cups, sugar—but sufficient. Hakim orders and drinks, watching the harbour reveal itself in strengthening light: fishing boats returning from night work, cargo ships awaiting permission to dock, yachts of the wealthy who weekend here, escaping Cairo's density for the coast's relative openness.

"You are Egyptian?" the vendor asks, though the question carries doubt.

"Yes, originally," Hakim answers, though yes simplifies, Egyptian has meant different things across his lifetime—Nasser's Arab socialism, Sadat's opening, Mubarak's stagnation, the revolution that failed or succeeded or both, depending on what one measures.

"But living outside," the vendor continues, not question but diagnosis, reading something in Hakim's posture, his clothes, his manner of holding the cup.

"Canada," Hakim concedes.

"Ah." The sound contains multitudes—envy, dismissal, understanding, incomprehension. The conversation ends. Other customers arrive. The day's commerce begins.

Hakim walks further east, the sun now climbing rapidly, or apparently rapidly. The Earth's rotation is constant, but our perception of it varies with attention, with the day's tasks, and with age. Children experience time dilated, stretched, each day containing eternities. Age compresses, accelerates, years passing like months once passed. Time's arrow—entropy manifesting in both subjective consciousness and universal expansion, the same directionality expressed at different scales. The universe's temperature declines asymptotically toward absolute zero, approachable but never reached.

The Corniche fills slowly with others: joggers whose

footfalls establish rhythm, elderly men with prayer beads whose fingers establish a different rhythm, women in groups whose conversations establish social rhythm. Alexandria waking, though waking suggests prior sleep and cities never sleep, only shift, only modulate, their consciousness distributed across millions of nodes, no central processor, no unified experience.

Looking back west, he can see how far he's walked—three kilometres, maybe four. The city spreads along the coast, apartment buildings of varying decay, some Ottoman, some colonial French, some Nasser-era concrete, some recent glass and steel, attempting Dubai's aesthetic without Dubai's capital. Layers of history coexisting uneasily, each era's ambitions partially realized, partially ruined. Like sedimentary rock, like tree rings, like the archaeological tells that dot this landscape, civilization accumulates vertically, each generation building on the previous' s rubble.

The sun is fully established now, its authority undeniable. Shadows sharpen, shorten, and will continue shortening until noon, when they nearly disappear, only to lengthen again toward evening. The day's arc is predictable, has been predicted since humans began observing patterns, recognizing cycles, creating calendars that are time made spatial, duration given form.

The dawn is complete, but dawn is never complete, always occurring somewhere as the Earth rotates, as the terminator—that line dividing day from night—sweeps westward at fifteen degrees longitude per hour. While I watched this dawn, others watched it from Crete, from Sicily, from the Balearics, the same sun from different angles, the same process differently witnessed. The Mediterranean doesn't experience dawn—it is the medium through which dawn is experienced, the surface that reflects, refracts, and makes visible what would otherwise be abstract celestial mechanics.

He closes the notebook, returns it to his pocket, where it travels with him like memory made material, like thought given weight. The pen, too, returns to its place, ink diminished by some millilitres, words extracted from liquid, meaning from matter. Neurons firing, synapses connecting, electrochemical cascades that are consciousness or produce consciousness or are produced by consciousness—the hard problem that philosophy hasn't solved, that perhaps cannot be solved from within consciousness. The eye is unable to see itself seeing.

A final look at the sea before turning back toward the city proper. It is fully blue now, that particular Mediterranean blue that is not the Atlantic's blue or the Pacific's blue or any lake's blue, but this blue, specific to this basin, this latitude, this mineral content, this history of seeing. Homer saw it wine-dark, perhaps at sunset, perhaps with eyes that parsed the spectrum differently, perhaps with language that categorized colour according to different principles. We see it blue and cannot see it otherwise, blue encoded in our expectations, our postcards, our memories, real and inherited.

The fisherman from earlier passes, his boat returning. "Good catch?" Hakim asks. "The sea was generous," the fisherman responds, the sea's generosity measured not in absolute catch but in the relationship between effort and reward, between risk and return. The fisherman continues toward wherever fish are sold, weighed, purchased, transformed from sea's gift to market's commodity. The economics of it: price per kilogram fluctuating with supply, demand, season, the invisible hand that Adam Smith imagined moving markets but which is really millions of visible hands exchanging currency for calories, for protein, for the taste of the sea on the tongue, salt and iodine and the particular sweetness of fresh fish that is not sweetness but its own category, umami before the Japanese named it, savory satisfaction that predates language.

Hakim walks back toward his apartment, toward the day that dawn has initiated but not determined. The streets are fuller now, Cairo's overflow, Alexandria's year-round residents, tourists beginning their documented adventures. Languages multiply: Arabic in its various dialects, English from the hotels, Russian from the new money, French from the old associations, Italian from those whose grandparents stayed when others left. The Mediterranean's linguistic diversity, Babel's legacy, or Babel's gift—the multiplication that prevents unity but enables diversity, that makes translation necessary, that keeps meaning in motion.

The sun climbs higher. The day heats. The sea continues its work of evaporation, condensation, and circulation. Somewhere, rain falls that was Mediterranean water, will be again. Somewhere, rivers flow toward this basin, carrying sediment, nutrients, pollutants, and history. The Nile, the Ebro, the Rhône, the Po—each contributing its particular chemistry, its particular story, to the sea that receives all, mixes all, returns all transformed.

Dawn is over, but not yet. Not this dawn. This dawn continues in its effects—the warmth that will build through the day, the light that will enable photosynthesis, vision, the reading of notebooks written in darkness, the interpretation of words that gesture toward meaning that exceeds language, that participates in the world's becoming while attempting to understand it.

The apartment building's entrance is shade, coolness, respite. Three flights up, reversing the morning's descent, feeling in his legs the labour that gravity demands, the work of lifting mass against acceleration, potential energy accumulating with each step. The door opens to the unfamiliar space, yesterday's arrival still fresh, still estranging. But something has shifted. The dawn walk has begun something—not transformation, too grand a word, but adjustment, calibration, the beginning of participation in Alexandria's rhythm, which is not his rhythm but might become the rhythm they create together, the pattern that emerges from their mutual engagement.

He sits at the small table on the balcony that faces the sea. From here, elevated, the Mediterranean spreads to the horizon, that line he stood before in darkness, now visible, now ordinary, now extraordinary again if attention permits, if the mind doesn't habituate, doesn't assume, doesn't take dawn for granted simply because it comes daily.

The notebook opens to the pages written in darkness. The words are legible, mostly, though some lines wander, overlap, and create palimpsests that require interpretation.

This, too, is appropriate—thought capturing itself imperfectly, meaning exceeding its inscription, the process continuing beyond its documentation.

Mediterranean dawn. Not possessive but participatory. I didn't observe the dawn—I participated in it, contributed my consciousness to its occurrence, was changed by it in ways I'm still discovering. The fisherman knew this, knew that the sea's generosity isn't separate from his attention to it, his skill in reading it, his submission to its patterns. Knowledge as participation, not extraction.

Tomorrow there will be another dawn. I won't see it—I'll participate in it or not, will be conscious or sleeping, will be alive or not, eventually not, certainly not. But the dawn doesn't require me. It requires only the Earth's rotation, the sun's combustion, and the atmosphere's mediation. My participation is contingent, temporary, and grateful. The process includes me today, will exceed me tomorrow or eventually tomorrow. This is not loss but location—finding one's place in processes larger than oneself, processes that were before consciousness, that will be after.

The pen stops. The morning is fully established. From the balcony, the Mediterranean has achieved its full blue, though full is always partial, though blue is always approximate, though achievement is always process, never product.

Time to close the notebook. Time to enter the day that dawn has made possible. Time to walk again, to participate again, to allow the city and sea to work their slow transformation on consciousness.

MORNING

Seven o'clock and the apartment has become a provisional shelter, its walls suddenly constrictive, the furniture suggesting domesticity that participatory consciousness cannot accept, not yet. The morning demands movement, not the dawn's tentative exploration but purposeful traversal, the city requiring witness at its full metabolic expression.

Hakim descends again—west this time, against the sun's trajectory, into light rather than following it. The reversal is not arbitrary; consciousness seeks what it hasn't yet encountered, the harbour leftward. The Corniche continues its arc, that limestone boundary between terrestrial and marine.

The city's morning metabolism expresses itself in diesel exhaust and bread scent, in the metallic percussion of shutters rising, in the polyphonic negotiation of traffic where lanes are suggestions rather than prescriptions. A different Alexandria than dawn revealed—not contemplative but commercial, not potential but kinetic.

The transformation is not merely temporal but ontological: the city that exists for consciousness at rest differs from the city that exists for consciousness in motion. Though *exists* is wrong, suggesting stability where there is only *process*.

He passes the Bibliotheca Alexandrina, that architectural assertion of recovered heritage, its disc-like structure tilted toward the Mediterranean as if listening for whispers from its drowned predecessor. Eleven floors, seven of them below ground—a building that burrows rather than soars, seeking foundation rather than elevation. The ancient library had no such architectural ambition. It was simply rooms, storage, the technology of papyrus and parchment, requiring no special environment beyond dryness and darkness when not being read. This new iteration, opened in 2002, attempts to materialize memory, to give form to absence, to make present what is irretrievably past.

The Library that burned—if it burned, the stories multiply and contradict—contained, they say, Aristotle's personal collection, the complete works of Aeschylus, Sophocles' 123 dramas of which we possess seven. Knowledge as commodity, hoarded, vulnerable to flame, to flood, to the simple entropy of organic molecules surrendering their bonds. But also: knowledge as pattern, surviving its material substrate. We have Euclid's Elements not from his hand but from copies of copies, each transmission introducing errors that become features, mutations that enable evolution. The new library cannot recover the old library's scrolls, but can continue its project—gathering, organizing, preserving, though preserving what? Not information, which proliferates beyond any institution's capacity. Perhaps preserving the idea of preservation itself.

Two tourists photograph themselves against the library's tilted wall, their poses practiced, immediate review on phone screens, deletion and repetition until the image satisfies some internal criterion. They speak German, or Swiss German, where the consonants are differently weighted. They don't enter the building—the photograph suffices, presence documented, Alexandria added to their collection of places possessed through images. Hakim, too, doesn't enter, but for different reasons, or perhaps the same reason differently articulated. To enter would be to accept the building's claim to continuity, its architectural argument that something persists across the centuries of absence. Better to pass, to acknowledge without affirming, to let the library exist in peripheral vision where it belongs, margin rather than center.

The harbour area begins to announce itself through olfactory gradient—salt concentration increasing, diesel mixing with marine decay, that particular combination that every working port produces, that globalizes the local even as it localizes the global. Container ships rest at anchor, their names declaring origins.

The ancient harbour lies beneath these waters, Cleopatra's palace among the submerged structures, though Cleopatra is a convenient designation for complex archaeological stratification. Marine archaeologists have mapped the ruins using sonar, photogrammetry, and technologies that reveal without exposing, that maintain the water's protective custody. Better preserved submerged than exposed to air, to tourism, to the particular violence of making the past present for consumption.

A café presents itself, or rather Hakim's trajectory intersects with its location, the encounter appearing inevitable retrospectively, though contingency governed each turn. Plastic chairs, aluminum tables, the universal furniture of provisional gathering. The proprietor is perhaps sixty, perhaps seventy, age becoming indefinite after certain thresholds, the body marking time differently, accumulated damage creating individual chronology. Hakim orders coffee—the man offers Nescafé, globalization's gift to caffeine delivery, instant satisfaction for those who accept approximation as equivalent.

"You are Egyptian?" the proprietor asks, the question becoming familiar, identity requiring constant verification.

"Originally," Hakim responds, originally containing both truth and evasion.

"But not currently," the man observes, not accusation but diagnosis.

"Canadian," Hakim concedes, though Canadian explains nothing, explains everything wrongly.

"The brain drain," the proprietor says in English, the phrase itself English, no Arabic equivalent carrying the same resignation mixed with pride—Egypt produces minds worthy of draining, even as their drainage diminishes what remains.

The coffee arrives, foam thick enough to support sugar briefly before molecular forces overcome structural integrity. Through the café's frame—it lacks walls, only posts supporting a corrugated roof—the Harbour curves, fishing boats returning though it's early still for their second departure. The two-cycle rhythm: pre-dawn for deep-water fish, late morning for different species, different depths, the sea stratified vertically as the city is stratified socially, each zone its own ecosystem, own rules, own possibilities.

A young woman enters, or appears—her movement too fluid for entry's mechanics. Perhaps twenty-five, lab coat over jeans, the costume of scientific authority adapted to contemporary casual. She orders in rapid Arabic, takes a table nearby, opens a laptop whose screen displays what Hakim recognizes as sequence data—the four-letter alphabet of nucleotides, ATCG, in combinations that encode existence.

"RNA sequencing?" he asks in English, the technical term lacking an Arabic equivalent, or rather, the Arabic would be translation, not native terminology.

She looks up, evaluates, and decides. "DNA, actually. Environmental sampling from the harbour." Her English carries British inflection overlaid on an Egyptian foundation, education's palimpsest.

"Marine biology?"

"Microbiology. We're mapping bacterial populations, how they've changed since—" she pauses, searching for euphemism or deciding against it, "—since the sewage treatment failures."

The conversation that follows is technical, professional,

the kind of exchange that transcends nationality through shared vocabulary and methodology. She's studying at Alexandria University, her project traces antibiotic resistance genes through marine environments, the harbour as a reservoir for genetic innovation, bacteria exchanging plasmids like ideas, and horizontal gene transfer enabling rapid adaptation.

"The Mediterranean is becoming a super-bacterial breeding ground," she explains, her tone clinical rather than alarmed. "Antibiotics from agricultural runoff, from human waste, from aquaculture—they create selective pressure. The bacteria that survive are increasingly resistant. We're watching evolution in real-time."

Evolution in real-time. The phrase lodges in consciousness, demands examination. Darwin imagined deep time, geological patience, and changes imperceptible within a human lifetime. But bacteria, with their twenty-minute generations, compress evolution into observable spans. The harbour she studies is not the harbour of last year, microbiologically speaking. Its bacterial population has adapted, incorporated new genes, and developed new resistances. Process philosophy made literal—identity through transformation, pattern persisting through material exchange.

"Like cancer," Hakim offers, his own expertise surfacing. "Leukemic cells evolving resistance to chemotherapy. The treatment creates selective pressure; the resistant clones proliferate."

"Exactly," she agrees, then pauses. "You're medical?"

"Was. Am." The tense confusion is accurate—he is credentialed, experienced, but not currently practicing, the knowledge persistent but dormant, like spores awaiting favourable conditions.

They discuss the parallel: blood as ecosystem, cancer as evolution, treatment as environmental pressure. The conversation ranges through molecular biology, evolutionary dynamics, and the philosophy of medicine, though neither names it as such. She mentions Canguilhem—*The Normal and the Pathological*—and he recognizes a kindred intelligence, someone who thinks beyond their discipline's boundaries, who recognizes those boundaries as provisional, porous.

"The fishermen hate our research," she mentions, gesturing toward the harbour. "We document what they don't want documented—the contamination, the declining fish stocks. They think we're bad for business."

"Are you?"

"Truth is bad for business if business depends on denial." She closes the laptop, preparing to leave. "But the sea doesn't care about business. It continues its processes. The bacteria adapt. The fish populations crash or recover. The chemistry changes. We just document, try to understand patterns."

She leaves without a formal goodbye, with scientific abruptness that assumes an ongoing conversation rather than a conclusion. Hakim remains, watches the harbour's morning commerce—boats departing and arriving, nets being repaired, the ancient rhythms persisting despite or through contemporary disruptions.

Knowledge circulates or stagnates. The ancient
library accumulated. Modern science reverses
this, generates data faster than comprehension,

and produces information that exceeds interpretation. The young scientist documents bacterial evolution, but what does it mean? The patterns she detects are real—genes spreading, resistance developing—but the pattern is not purpose. Evolution has no telos, no direction, only response to pressure. The Mediterranean becomes a reservoir for resistance genes—so? The bacteria don't care. The sea doesn't care. Only consciousness cares, and consciousness is a recent addition, perhaps temporary, certainly not necessary for the processes to continue.

A swimmer appears, unexpected at this hour, at this location—not the tourist beaches eastward but here among the working boats, the diesel slicks, the documented contamination. An older man, perhaps Hakim's age, entering the water with practiced economy, no hesitation at temperature or chemistry. He swims parallel to shore, steady crawl, breathing rhythm synchronized with stroke, the body's mechanics refined through repetition into something approaching efficiency, though efficiency in water is always relative, humans being terrestrial adaptations momentarily returning to ancestral medium.

The swimmer continues, perhaps half a kilometre, then returns, emerges, towels himself with the same economy that marked entry. He notices Hakim watching, "You swim?" the man asks, though the question carries invitation rather than inquiry.

"Not here." The qualification acknowledges the possibility without commitment.

"The water is polluted, they say. Bacteria, heavy metals, microplastics." The man towels his hair, casual about contamination. "But I've been swimming here for twenty-five years. My body and the harbour have reached accommodation. We've evolved together."

The statement carries scientific precision despite conversational delivery. Evolution, accommodation—the vocabulary suggests education beyond casual usage.

"You're visiting?" the swimmer asks, reading something in Hakim's observational stance, his particular quality of attention.

"Recently arrived." The explanation invites further query.

"For work? Research?" the man asks.

"Something like that." Hakim's response is both accurate and evasive.

"I teach mathematics," the swimmer adds. "Secondary school, here in Alexandria. Though mathematics is philosophy by other means—patterns, relationships, the structures that persist through transformation."

They shake hands. "You came to Alexandria specifically, not Cairo, where opportunities are, Alexandria—the city of departure, nostalgia. Why?"

"The philosophical tradition," Hakim offers.

"The mythology," the man interrupts, not unkindly. "Everyone comes for the mythology. Foreigners seeking the cosmopolitan past, Egyptians seeking escape from the present. Both disappointed."

A pause while a delivery truck passes, diesel exhaust thick. Both men wait without covering faces, accepting the air as they accept the water.

"You chose to come," the man says. "That's different from returning. Those who return seek what was. Those who choose seek what might be. The distinction matters."

"And those who stay?"

"We seek nothing. We simply continue. Teaching mathematics to children who will leave, swimming in water that worsens, watching the city proceed through its processes. It's not resignation—it's participation without illusion."

They discuss the paradox—Hakim chose Alexandria for its philosophical significance, but the man remains despite its philosophical emptiness. One seeks meaning in a city that's become pure process, the other continues process in a city drained of meaning.

"The students I teach, they dream of Europe, anywhere but here. How to explain that Alexandria teaches through its failures what success cannot—that entropy is as philosophical as construction, that decline reveals structures, growth conceals?"

"You make it sound like a conscious choice rather than a circumstance."

"Everything is circumstance reframed as choice, or choice revealed as circumstance. The distinction collapses in practice." He mounts a bicycle and cycles away.

Hakim continues westward, but the encounter has shifted something. Not recognition of shared past but acknowledgment of different relationships to the same present. The teacher participates through repetition, Hakim through observation. Both are valid methods of engaging processes that include consciousness.

Walking now with different attention—not seeking what

he'd read and imagined about Alexandria but observing what Alexandria has become. The contemporary city that continues despite scholarly projection, that offers no validation for philosophical fantasy, that processes contamination and consciousness with equal indifference.

Persistence through repetition, not progress. The phrase articulates something essential about place, about staying, about the difference between those who leave and those who remain. Hakim sought progress—medical advancement, career trajectory, and the immigrant's faith in transformation. The teacher accepted repetition—teaching the children, swimming in progressively polluted water, watching Alexandria simultaneously decay and develop. Neither choice is superior, but they produce different consciousnesses, different relationships to time and to change.

Walking westward still, the sun now high enough to create sharp shadows, the morning's gold light whitening toward noon's harsh illumination. The harbour continues its arc, industrial facilities replacing fishing boats, the scale shifting from artisanal to corporate. Cranes load containers with mechanical precision, the global supply chain's local node, goods from China trans-shipping to Europe, African raw materials heading toward Asian processing, the circulation that capitalism calls efficiency, but which is really entropy accelerated, resources converted to waste via commodity.

He thinks of blood's circulation, that metaphor that is not a metaphor but a structural echo. Arterial blood carries oxygen, nutrients, toward tissues that consume, that produce waste, that return venous blood depleted, requiring pulmonary renewal, cardiac propulsion, the cycle continuing until it doesn't. The global economy circulates similarly—resources extracted, processed, consumed, discarded, the waste accumulating in places like this harbour, in futures like the young scientist documents without judgment, with clinical precision that masks or reveals despair.

A vendor offers fish, this morning's catch displayed on ice that melts steadily, entropy made visible. The fish are small—no large predators anymore, those populations collapsed from overfishing, only the species that reproduce quickly, that adapt to disruption. Ecological simplification, diversity surrendering to resilience, or what appears as resilience but might be system failure's early stage. The vendor calls prices, reduces them as Hakim passes without stopping, the commerce of necessity, selling before spoilage, before the ice becomes water, before the morning's harvest becomes afternoon's waste.

The Mediterranean as an ecosystem is dying, has been dying since humans began concentrating along its shores, will continue dying until it doesn't, until it transforms into something else, some other configuration of chemistry and biology. Death is transformation, not termination. The ancient library died, but knowledge continued elsewhere. The Roman Empire died, but Latin persisted in evolved forms. Species die, but their genes continue in descendants or don't, ending being as real as continuance. Process philosophy accommodates both—not everything persists, not every pattern continues. Some processes conclude. The difficulty is distinguishing conclusion from transformation while still within the process.

Noon approaches, and the heat is building toward its daily maximum. The morning walk has covered perhaps six kilometres, a trivial distance globally but significant locally, each meter carrying specific history, specific possibility. The harbour curves back toward the Corniche, toward the apartment, though return is not retreat but completion of circuit, the path that enables comprehension of territory, that transforms space into place through embodied knowledge.

Near the Corniche's resumption, where the harbour yields to open sea, a small group has gathered around something invisible from a distance. Approaching, Hakim discovers a sea turtle, dead, washed ashore during the night. *Caretta caretta*, the loggerhead, once common here, is now endangered, this individual's death adding to population statistics that trend toward zero. The turtle is perhaps a meter long, mass maybe thirty kilograms, the shell intact but flesh beginning decomposition's work, bacteria and heat collaborating in material recycling.

A child asks why it died. The mother responds with comforting fiction—old age, natural causes. But visible plastic emerges from the throat, a bag or wrapper that mimics jellyfish in water, that turtles consume, that blocks digestion, that kills slowly through starvation, while the stomach fills with petroleum products. The child doesn't see or doesn't understand the plastic's significance. The mother sees, understands, and chooses silence's mercy.

Someone calls authorities—the turtle will be removed, disposed of, its death becoming a statistic if recorded, anecdote if not. The crowd disperses, the morning's rhythm resuming, the incident already becoming memory, story, the turtle transformed from biological entity to narrative element, its material existence concluded but its symbolic presence just beginning, rippling through consciousness like waves through water, each witness carrying the image forward, modified, interpreted, incorporated into different frameworks of meaning.

Hakim photographs the turtle with his phone, the digital image reducing three dimensions to two, colour to pixels, death to documentation. Why? The question arises after the action, the documentation preceding the purpose. Evidence? Memory? The photograph exists now in the phone's memory, will be uploaded to cloud storage, will persist in servers consuming electricity generated perhaps from natural gas extracted from beneath this very sea, the cycles of extraction and consumption so complex that causation becomes untraceable, responsibility diffuse, everything connected but nothing accountable.

The turtle's death is not a metaphor but a fact. Its species' decline is not symbolic but a measurable population collapse. The plastic in its throat is not human malice but systemic indifference, the externalities of convenience aggregating into extinction. Yet consciousness cannot encounter death without making meaning, cannot witness the ending without seeking pattern. The turtle becomes Mediterranean's condition made visible— ancient species succumbing to contemporary chemistry, evolution outpaced by industrial transformation, deep time intersecting with accelerated time at this point on this beach where this child asks why and this mother responds with necessary fiction while truth decomposes in sunlight.

The walk continues, must continue, movement being consciousness's mode of processing, integration through ambulation. The sun approaches zenith, shadows contracting toward vanishing point, the day pivoting from morning to afternoon, though the transition is conceptual, imposed, the sun's movement being continuous, our categorization being convenience.

Returning toward the apartment but not yet ready for enclosure, Hakim finds another café, this one elevated, offering harbour view, tourist prices, the location's value extracted through economic rent. He orders water, not coffee, as hydration becomes necessary as the temperature exceeds the body's baseline. The water arrives in a plastic bottle—a company that claims water rights globally, that commodifies what was common, that profits from the enclosure of necessity. He drinks despite or through the contradiction, participation requiring compromise, purity being impossible, complicity being the condition of contemporary existence.

From this elevation, the harbour reveals its organization—zones of activity, patterns of movement, the syntax of maritime commerce. Fishing boats occupy the eastern section, their scale human, comprehensible. Cargo ships dominate the western section, their scale exceeding human proportion, sublime in the technical sense— awareness of magnitude that consciousness cannot fully accommodate. Between them, yachts cluster, the leisure class's vessels, mobility as luxury, the sea as playground rather than workplace.

The young scientist's words return: evolution in real-time. Not just bacterial but cultural, economic, and ecological. The harbour evolving from an ancient trade center to a modern industrial port to future uncertainty— climate change raising sea levels, temperature, acidity, the conditions that enabled this city's existence shifting beyond historical parameters. Alexandria, like all coastal cities, faces submersion, not immediately but inevitably, the ice sheets' stored water returning to liquid, seeking level, reclaiming what was always borrowed, temporarily emerged, the land's appearance above water being an exception, not a rule, in Earth's biography.

Morning concludes, though morning never concludes, somewhere dawn is breaking as here noon approaches, the planet's rotation ensuring continuity, ensuring change, ensuring that no moment persists, that every configuration is temporary. I have walked perhaps eight kilometres, have encountered perhaps a hundred people, and have exchanged words with some. The morning has taught what morning teaches: that the city continues, that knowledge circulates, that evolution proceeds indifferent to evaluation, that processes include us temporarily, that participation is not optional but only more or less conscious, more or less intentional. The harbour's polluted water will continue receiving swimmers, boats, and drainage. The library will continue asserting continuity. The turtle will be removed, but others will die, wash ashore, will be witnessed, and will become a story. None of this matters. All of this matters. Both statements true, neither complete, the paradox being not logical failure but accurate description of consciousness encountering world, making meaning from processes that exceed meaning, that preceded consciousness, that will continue when the last synapse fires its final signal, when the last book closes, when the last swimmer emerges from the sea that doesn't notice, doesn't care, doesn't stop.

The notebook closes. The pen returns to the pocket. The water bottle, emptied, remains on the table, its plastic persisting for centuries, breaking into smaller pieces but never disappearing, becoming microplastic that fish consume, that enters food chains, that circulates through bodies like the teacher's, like the child who asked about the turtle, the material trace of this moment's hydration spreading through space and time in patterns too complex to track but real nonetheless.

Time to return to the apartment to process what the morning has provided—encounters, recognitions, the city revealing itself through traversal, through participation, through the consciousness that walking enables, that sitting prevents, that makes the philosopher peripatetic by necessity, not choice.

NOON

Noon: when shadows contract to nothing, when the sun occupies zenith, when Alexandria becomes what Durrell called "the white city," though white is absence, all wavelengths reflected, nothing absorbed, the city refusing light rather than accepting it.

Hakim, at another café, has chosen the table furthest from others, a corner position that enables observation while minimizing exposure—the anthropologist's location, the clinician's remove, though remove is fiction, consciousness always implicated in what it witnesses. The notebook lies open, pages bright enough to hurt, the pen's shadow the only mark until writing begins. Around him, the café's other occupants have arranged themselves according to social geometries he recognizes but doesn't enter: the businessmen conducting what business remains possible in Alexandria's economic constraints, the women whose leisure is performance, carefully constructed, the solitary man whose solitude differs from Hakim's—not chosen but imposed, isolation rather than withdrawal.

The waiter brings water without being asked—noon demands hydration, the body's water content requiring constant replenishment as perspiration attempts thermal regulation. The glass sweats immediately, condensation forming as water vapour meets surface cooled below the dew point, phase transition made visible. Hakim drinks, replaces loss, maintains the hydrochemical balance that enables consciousness, that seven-tenths water composition that makes humans marine organisms temporarily terrestrialized, carrying ocean within, salt concentration in blood matching ancient seas, evolution's memory written in sodium chloride.

Alexandria: founded by Alexander, who came from Macedonia to conquer Egypt, who died in Babylon at thirty-two, whose body was brought here, displayed in a gold sarcophagus, then a glass one, then lost. The city begins in conquest, a foreign imposition that becomes native through duration, through forgetting. Ptolemaic dynasty: Greek pharaohs ruling Egypt for three centuries, Cleopatra the last, her suicide, Rome's victory, Augustus making Egypt personal property, bread basket, the Nile's fertility feeding the empire. Then Byzantium, a brief Persian interlude, the Arab conquest that brings Islam, that makes Egypt Arabic, though Egypt was never Arab before, becomes Arab through linguistic conversion, religious transformation, cultural conquest that calls itself liberation.

The pen moves across paper, thought becoming mark, mark becoming memory external to biological substrate, the notebook as prosthetic consciousness, extending mind beyond skull's boundaries.

Napoleon arrived in 1798, bringing scientists, linguists, and the Description de l'Égypte, which made Egypt an object of European knowledge, possession through documentation. Then Muhammad Ali, an Albanian mercenary who became Ottoman viceroy, became an autonomous ruler, a modernizer whose modernization means debt, means European capital penetrating the Egyptian economy. The British bombardment of 1882, the protectorate that protects British interests, and the Suez Canal as the jugular vein of the empire. Independence that isn't, a monarchy that serves foreign capital, revolution 1952, Nasser's Arab socialism that builds the High Dam, that nationalizes the canal, that makes Egypt the center of Arab consciousness briefly, before defeat, before Sadat's reversal, before the present.

Each conquest presents itself as liberation. Alexander liberates from Persian rule. Rome liberates from Ptolemaic decay. Arabs liberate from Byzantine oppression. Napoleon liberates from Mamluk stagnation. British liberate from Oriental despotism. Nasser liberates from colonial subjugation. Each liberation becomes a new form of constraint. The pattern doesn't progress—it repeats with variations, like musical theme transposed through different keys, same structure, different tonal center.

The writing pauses. Through the café's shade, the noon sun creates a sharp boundary, bisecting the floor, dividing space into habitable and uninhabitable zones. A cat sleeps exactly at the boundary, half in shade, half in sun, the body's thermoregulation more sophisticated than conscious calculation, finding precisely the thermal equilibrium that enables maximum rest with minimum effort.

Two tourists enter, their skin already reddening from morning exposure, melanin insufficient for this latitude's ultraviolet intensity. They photograph themselves with a sea backdrop, discuss in loud voices their itinerary—the catacombs this afternoon, Pompey's Pillar tomorrow, the standard circuit that reduces Alexandria to its monuments, its dead history, missing the living city that continues despite or through tourism's extractive attention. They see Hakim writing, assume he's local, and ask in broken English for restaurant recommendations. He responds minimally, returns to the notebook before the conversation can establish itself.

Process philosophy accommodates benign processes too easily—growth, development, creative advance. But processes include degradation, exploitation, and forced participation. The slave trade was a process— human bodies circulated through the Atlantic system, transformed from persons to property to profit. Colonialism was a process—resources extracted, value transferred, metropolitan centers enriched through peripheral impoverishment. These processes created patterns that persist. Alexandria's wealth came from controlling trade between Europe and Asia, extracting rent from its geographic position. The wealth concentrated, displayed in palaces now submerged, while the peasants continued their seasonal cycles, their surplus appropriated by whatever dynasty claimed ownership.

Cancer is a process—cells proliferating without constraint, circulation becoming metastasis, growth becoming pathology. In leukemia, blood cells forget their differentiation, return to a primitive state, multiply without purpose, and crowd out functional cells. The process continues until it doesn't, until chemotherapy's violence interrupts, or until the organism fails. Not all processes deserve continuation. Some require interruption, cessation, the difficult decision to stop what has begun, to refuse participation.

A family arrives at a nearby table—parents, two children, the domestic geometry that reproduces itself across cultures with variations in configuration but consistent in function. The children are perhaps eight and ten, the age where boredom is voiced rather than endured. They want to swim, to move, to be elsewhere. The parents want rest, shade, the pause that child-rearing rarely permits. The negotiation proceeds in Arabic fast enough that Hakim catches only fragments—promises, threats, the eventual compromise that satisfies no one but enables continuation.

The mother notices Hakim watching, offers an apologetic smile, the international gesture of parental exhaustion. He responds with a slight nod, acknowledgment without engagement, the interaction complete in its brevity. She returns to managing her children's energy, their bodies that reject stillness, that demand activity, that haven't yet learned capitalism's discipline of sitting, waiting, enduring.

The sea witnesses but doesn't judge. It received Phoenician traders and Roman galleys with equal indifference. It carried slaves from Africa and grain to Rome, the commercial traffic that makes atrocity routine. During the Second World War, it became a battlefield—Rommel and Montgomery, Afrika Korps and Desert Rats, the Mediterranean campaign that determined whether fascism or liberal democracy would control these waters, though for the colonized, the distinction was minimal, both systems extracting, both maintaining hierarchy through violence monopolized by the state.

Now it receives refugees—displaced seeking Europe's promise, finding often the sea's depth instead. The drownings number in thousands annually, bodies unrecovered, unmarked, the Mediterranean becomes a cemetery, an archive of attempted crossing. The boats are overloaded, engines insufficient, navigation by phone until batteries die, then stars, then hope, then nothing. Frontex patrols with thermal cameras, satellites track movement, the sea is surveilled but not secured, and the processes of displacement continue despite or because of intervention.

The pen stops. The hand cramps from sustained writing, muscles fatigued, tendons inflamed. Hakim flexes fingers, rotates wrist, the small movements that restore circulation, that prevent repetitive stress injury, the occupational hazard of thought made material through inscription. The notebook remains open, the words visible but increasingly difficult to read in the sun's harsh light, the contrast between white paper and black ink diminishing as pupils contract, as eyes strain to maintain focus.

The waiter brings coffee—though Hakim didn't order it, the assumption that noon coffee is necessary, is ritual, is what consciousness requires to persist through the day's heat. The small cup arrives with a glass of water, the pairing essential, caffeine's dehydration countered by parallel hydration, the body's chemistry maintained in an acceptable range through simultaneous opposing inputs.

Violence is not a deviation from process—it is process, one among many, neither exceptional nor necessary, simply possible, often actual. The scorpion stings because its evolution equipped it with venom, not from malice but from process, pattern, the successful strategy reproduced. Humans developed the capacity for organized violence—weapons, armies, and the transformation of technology into force projection. This too is a process, neither good nor evil, categories that consciousness imposes but that processes don't recognize.

The ethical question is not whether to participate; participation is a given, involuntary condition of existence. The question is how to participate, with what degree of consciousness, toward what ends if ends exist, which process philosophy questions, denying teleology while unable to escape it entirely, consciousness being apparently purposive even if purpose is projection, interpretation, the meaning-making that distinguishes awareness from mere process.

Through the café's opening, the harbour is visible in partial view, the angle revealing a commercial dock where containers accumulate, their colours—red, blue, green—the only variation in industrial monotony. Each container is a standardized unit, twenty or forty feet, the dimensions that rationalize global trade, that make all ports equivalent, interchangeable, the specificities of place erased by logistics' requirements. Alexandria's harbour could be Rotterdam, Singapore, Los Angeles—the same cranes, same containers, same conversion of geography into a network node.

A ship is being unloaded, or loaded—from this distance, the direction of flow is invisible. The crane moves with mechanical precision, each container taking perhaps few minutes from ship to shore or shore to ship, the rhythm hypnotic, industrial process at its most refined, human labor minimized, mostly eliminated, the dock workers who once made ports centers of radical politics replaced by operators in air-conditioned cabins, pushing buttons, moving joysticks, their bodies protected from heat, from weather, from the material reality of what they move.

Capital accumulates through circulation, Marx observed, though observed is wrong—he diagnosed, analyzed, performed conceptual surgery on capitalism's logic. The commodity must move to realize value, must transform from product to money to product again, the cycle accelerating with each technical innovation. Containerization was such an innovation—reducing loading time from days to hours, eliminating theft, and standardizing handling. The sea adapted, ports dredged deeper, ships enlarged, economies of scale pursued until ships became too large.

The Mediterranean is marginal now in global shipping—neither Pacific nor Atlantic volume, neither Chinese production nor American consumption at a sufficient scale. It serves regional trade, tourism, the movement of people deemed illegal, weapons deemed necessary, and drugs deemed profitable despite or because of prohibition. The sea that was once the center is now the periphery, though center and periphery are relative, positional; the view from Alexandria is different from that from Brussels, from Damascus, from Tripoli.

The tourists have left, payment left on the table, tip insufficient by local standards, but they don't know, won't learn, will repeat the error at each establishment, their ignorance protected by economic asymmetry, their euros worth enough that precision doesn't matter. The waiter clears their table without expression, the tip disappearing into a pocket, the accumulation of small amounts that might, aggregated, enable something—rent payment, medical procedure, child's education, the investments in future that poverty makes difficult, sometimes impossible.

The family continues their negotiation, the children's energy temporarily contained by phones, screens pacifying what parental authority couldn't, the devices that transform children into consumers of content, attention harvested, data extracted, behavioural patterns analyzed, predicted, modified through algorithmic intervention. The parents, too, consult phones, the family together but separate, each consciousness interfacing with a different network, different flow of information, the table they share merely physical proximity, not social unity.

The heat is fact, not metaphor. Thirty-seven degrees Celsius in shade, higher in the sun, humidity from the sea making evaporative cooling inefficient. The body responds—vasodilation, perspiration, behavioural adaptation (seeking shade, reducing movement). But sustained heat stress degrades cognitive function, increases irritability, correlates with violence, the summer murder rate exceeding winter's, the temperature's effect on consciousness is measurable, predictable, and ignored in discussions of political violence that prefer ideological explanation to thermodynamic.

Climate change will make Alexandria uninhabitable, not immediately but within a century, probably sooner. A sea level rise of two meters, the conservative projection, submerges the Corniche, the harbour. But before submersion, heat—wet bulb temperatures exceeding thirty-five degrees, the threshold beyond which human bodies cannot cool themselves, when perspiration fails, when shade provides no relief, when even rest becomes lethal. The wealthy will migrate, have already begun, to their properties in cooler latitudes, their mobility purchased. The poor will remain, will adapt until adaptation fails, will die in place, their deaths statistics in reports that recommend mitigation, adaptation, resilience, the language that admits defeat without acknowledging responsibility.

Hakim closes the notebook, the writing becoming forced, the thoughts too dark for noon's harsh light, though darkness and light are not opposed but complementary, the full spectrum necessary for vision, for comprehension, for the honest account that participatory philosophy demands if it's to be more than academic exercise, more than comfortable abstraction that avoids violence, suffering, the processes that consciousness wishes weren't but are.

Standing brings vertigo, brief but concerning—the heat's effect, dehydration despite water consumed, the body announcing its limits, its objection to conditions that consciousness chose but that cellular processes didn't, couldn't, evolution not anticipating air conditioning's absence, the body expecting technological mediation that isn't available, not here, not now.

The walk to the apartment will be brief but difficult, the sun at zenith making every surface radiate, the city becomes a furnace, the air itself seemingly solid, resistant, requiring effort to traverse. But traverse he must, the alternative being continued sitting, continued exposure, the heat accumulating in the body until systems fail, until consciousness retreats, until the processes that enable awareness cease their coordination.

The Mediterranean doesn't care. This phrase recurs because it's true. After all, consciousness projects care onto a world that doesn't reciprocate, that continues its processes indifferent to meaning, to suffering, to the beauty and horror consciousness discovers, creates, and endures. The sea will outlast Alexandria, will outlast humanity, will continue until Earth's water evaporates as the sun expands, becomes a red giant, makes this planet what Venus is now—greenhouse beyond life's tolerance, the processes of chemistry continuing without biology, without consciousness, without witness.

But consciousness does care, can't not care, the meaning-making compulsion that might be error, might be gift, might be simply what this configuration of matter does under these conditions, for this duration, until it doesn't. To care without reciprocation, to make meaning in a meaningless universe, to continue despite futility—this too is process, perhaps the most difficult, certainly the most human, possibly the most temporary.

He walks toward the apartment, the street's heat shimmer making the buildings appear to undulate, solid become liquid, the phase transition that heat suggests but doesn't actually accomplish, the buildings remaining solid despite appearance, the permanence that is not permanent but persistent enough for human purposes, for the fiction of stability that civilization requires, that consciousness assumes despite knowing better.

The sea remains visible peripherally, its noon blue now white with glare, painful to perceive directly, the

Mediterranean at its least accommodating, its least romantic, its most honest—not the wine-dark sea of poetry but the bright burning surface that reflects rather than absorbs, that makes vision painful, that reminds consciousness of its limits, its vulnerability, its temporary permission to witness processes that preceded it, that continue through it, that will persist beyond it.

A door opens—shade, stairs, ascent to apartment that waits, that provides shelter, that enables continuation through afternoon's heat toward evening's promise of cooling, of softening light, of the day's arc continuing toward conclusion that is not conclusion but transition, darkness returning, the cycle continuing, the process that includes this consciousness today, temporarily, gratefully, despite everything, because of everything.

The apartment door closes behind him. The heat remains outside, mostly. The shutters remain closed, maintaining darkness that is cooler than light, the simple physics of radiation and absorption, the strategies that predate air conditioning, that make life possible at this latitude, this season, this moment in the anthropocene that is ending the holocene, that is creating new processes, new patterns, new forms of suffering and possibly, not certainly, new forms of consciousness adequate to what comes next, what is already arriving, what cannot be stopped only witnessed, endured, possibly survived.

He drinks water, sits, opens the notebook again, and reads what was written in the café's harsh light. The words remain, the thoughts fixed in ink, the morning's meditation on power, violence, the dark processes that participatory philosophy must acknowledge if it is to be honest, if it is to be more than consolation, more than evasion, more than the academic exercise that makes suffering abstract, manageable, publishable.

Noon teaches what noon teaches: that maximum illumination creates maximum shadow, that seeing everything means seeing nothing, that the body has limits consciousness ignores at its peril, that the sea continues indifferent to witness, that processes include violence as surely as they include growth, that participation is not always voluntary, that some processes require interruption, that others continue despite our wish they wouldn't, that consciousness makes meaning from meaninglessness, that this might be error or gift or simply what happens when matter organizes at this level of complexity, for this duration, in this place, at this time, under this sun that burns without malice, that gives life and death with equal indifference, that makes possible the very consciousness that questions it, that will outlast the questions, the questioner, the questioned, everything except the process itself, which has no name, needs no name, continues without naming.

The pen stops. The notebook closes. Noon passes into afternoon, the sun beginning its descent from zenith.

AFTERNOON

Two o'clock and the heat has achieved what physicists call steady state—maximum sustained intensity without further increase, the sun's angle beginning its decline from zenith, but radiation accumulated in stone, in asphalt, in the city's material substrate continuing to emit, the urban heat island effect.

Hakim emerges from the apartment into heat that has weight, presence, almost personality—malevolent but not personal, the malevolence of physics, of thermodynamics pursuing equilibrium through consciousness's discomfort. The body adapts, must adapt, vasodilation increasing, pulse quickening to maintain circulation despite blood vessels' expansion, the cardiovascular system working harder to achieve what cool air enables without effort.

Each step requires decision, commitment, the will to continue despite cellular objection, despite evolutionary programming that says seek shade, reduce activity, wait for evening's cooling that will come, must come, has always come, though always is brief in geological time, climate being variable across scales consciousness barely comprehends.

West again, but further than morning's circuit. The streets narrow as he moves inland from the Corniche, away from tourist Alexandria, from cosmopolitan pretensions, toward the Alexandria he'd imagined from reading Durrell's city, Cavafy's, the philosophical capital that existed more in text than territory.

Hakim walked into the Alexandria that Alexandrians inhabit when not performing for a foreign gaze. Laundry hangs between buildings, a semaphore of domestic life, clothes drying in heat that evaporates water faster than sun bleaches colour. Children play football in an alley, the ball improvised from plastic bags wrapped with string, the goal marked by sandals, the game proceeding according to rules both universal and local, disputes resolved through volume rather than authority.

He passes a mosque, not historic, not notable, one of thousands that punctuate the city, that make sacred space from ordinary architecture. The afternoon call to prayer has passed, or has not yet arrived, temporal orientation becoming uncertain in the heat that makes duration elastic. Through an open doorway, darkness that promises coolness, men arranging themselves on carpets, the geometric precision of prayer that makes community from individual bodies, that synchronizes consciousness through synchronized posture.

The notebook remains in the apartment, but consciousness continues its inscription, thought proceeding through internal dialogue, the self split into observer and observed, the doubling that enables reflection but prevents presence, always already removed from immediate experience by the gap that consciousness is, or creates, or suffers.

A building presents itself—the balconies' pattern, their wrought iron baroque, despite the building's otherwise minimal ornamentation. An old man sits in the doorway's shade, watching without seeming to watch, the surveillance that the elderly perform in neighbourhoods worldwide, the informal security that knows who belongs, who doesn't, who might be. Hakim approaches, Arabic rusty but functional, asks about the building's history, carefully indirect, the circumlocution that politeness requires.

They discuss the neighbourhood's changes—the new shopping center that displaced the informal market, the school that closed, then reopened as a language institute, the mosque that expanded, consuming adjacent buildings. The man has witnessed it all, recorded nothing, his memory the only archive, unreliable, precious, disappearing with each death, each departure.

"The sea doesn't change," the man says eventually, perhaps a conversational formula, perhaps a deeper recognition that while human constructions transform, the Mediterranean persists, its cycles longer than human generations, its memory written in currents, temperatures, chemistry rather than consciousness.

Hakim continues walking, fewer shops, more life lived rather than commercialized. Women talk between doorways, their conversation pausing as he passes, resuming with slight modulation, his presence noted, incorporated, accommodated without welcome or rejection, the neutrality that urban density requires, enables, enforces. Children everywhere—school being out, or not in session, or truancy tolerated in the heat that makes learning impossible. They play games whose rules emerge from play itself, disputes arising, resolving, arising again, and the social learning that precedes formal education, which might be more essential.

The afternoon continues its arc toward evening, the sun lowering, the shadows beginning to lengthen though still harsh, still sharp, the light that reveals texture, detail, the accumulated damage that surfaces bear—weather, use, time's passage written in material degradation. He walks without destination now, the search abandoned or fulfilled through abandonment, each street equally meaningful or meaningless, the city revealing itself as present reality, what exists now, what continues despite or through transformation.

A sound draws attention—splashing, laughter, the acoustic signature of water play. Following it leads to a small square where children swim in a fountain not designed for swimming, their bodies adapting the space to their needs, the official purpose subverted, superseded. They jump from the fountain's edge, perhaps meter high, the water perhaps meter deep, the danger minimal but real, the risk that makes play meaningful, that distinguishes it from entertainment, from the supervised safety that privilege provides, demands.

The children are of various ages, maybe six to twelve, the older ones monitoring the younger without seeming to, the informal care that communities provide when formal structures fail or never existed. Their joy is uncomplicated, or seems so from the outside, from an adult perspective that reads joy where it might be simple cooling, simple occupation of time that must be occupied somehow.

One boy, perhaps ten, executes a backwards flip, the motion practiced, perfected, performed for applause that comes from his peers, from watching adults, from the city that needs joy, that takes it where found. He climbs out, prepares to repeat, notices Hakim watching, performs again with slight exaggeration, the showing off that childhood permits, requires, the establishment of identity through demonstrated capability.

An old man sits on a bench near the fountain, watching the children with an expression that might be simple attendance without evaluation. Hakim sits at the bench's other end, the distance calibrated—close enough for potential conversation, far enough to avoid obligation. They watch together, the children's energy seemingly infinite though finite, obviously, entropy applies to play as to all processes.

"Every afternoon," the man says eventually, Arabic slow, clear, accommodating Hakim's foreign presence without acknowledging it.

"The same children?"

"Some same, some different. The fountain is constant."

The fountain is constant. The phrase carries weight beyond its simplicity—the fixed point around which variation orbits, the stability that enables change, the stage that remains while actors transform.

"You have grandchildren among them?"

"No. My children left. Germany, two. America, one. They have children I've seen only in photographs. Digital. The phone shows me grandchildren I'll never touch."

The statement is matter-of-fact, loss presented without sentiment, the global dispersion of families that modernity enables, requires, and normalizes. The man's children succeeded, escaped, abandoned—all terms accurate, none complete.

"You stayed."

"Someone must stay. The city requires witnesses. Otherwise, it's just buildings. The children—" he gestures toward the fountain, "—they don't know they're keeping Alexandria alive. They think they're just swimming. But without them, what is the city? Museums? Hotels? The stones the tourists photograph? The city is this—children in fountains, illegally, temporarily, necessarily."

The city requires witnesses. The phrase articulates something essential about place, about duration, about the difference between space and place. Space is coordinates, geometry, the abstract grid that mapping imposes. Place is lived, witnessed, the accumulation of moments that consciousness attends to, that memory preserves however inaccurately, that creates meaning from mere matter. Alexandria has been witnessed for two millennia, continuously if not consistently, the witnesses changing but witnessing continuing, the city persisting through being perceived, through participating in consciousness that participates in it.

The children tire, finally, their energy depleted or

redirected. They disperse, the fountain returning to its official function—decoration, civic beautification, the water circulating without purpose beyond circulation itself. The old man walks away without goodbye, the interaction complete, its wisdom delivered or received or both or neither, the words continuing to resonate as Hakim remains seated, watching the empty fountain, the water that continues its circulation, its process, indifferent to observation.

The light is changing rapidly now, the sun perhaps an hour from the horizon, the shadows long, the heat beginning its barely perceptible decrease. Time to walk again, to move toward evening, toward the day's next phase, the continuation that is not repetition but variation, the same structure with different content, the pattern that persists through transformation.

Hakim rises and walks toward the Corniche, which appears with the sea beyond it gold now, the sun low enough that looking is possible though still difficult, the glare decreased but not eliminated. He could continue to the apartment, could rest before evening's walk, but momentum carries him forward, toward the sea that has been the destination, the background, the constant through the day's variations.

At the sea wall, different from morning's position, different light revealing different surface, he stops, watches, the simple attention that asks nothing, expects nothing, receives what is given—waves, light, the intersection of fluid and electromagnetic radiation that creates what we call beauty though beauty is category imposed, not inherent, the sea being neither beautiful nor ugly but simply what it is, process continuing, pattern persisting. The Mediterranean that has been here, will be here, until it isn't, until conditions change beyond the parameters that allow liquid water, that permit seas, that enable consciousness to perceive, to name, to assign meaning that the sea neither acknowledges nor refuses, simply continues through, despite, because of, the categories becoming irrelevant against the fact of water moving, always moving, the circulation that defines sea as different from lake, from pond, from the contained water that stagnates, that dies, while the sea continues, connects, circulates, the process that includes everything, excludes nothing, continues regardless.

EVENING

Six o'clock and the sun has begun its calculated descent. The Corniche has become a theatre, a stage for evening's performance, the daily gathering that makes public space social space, that transforms geography into community, temporarily, provisionally.

Hakim walks westward now, the sea to his right has begun its chromatic sequence—the blue deepening, complexifying, becoming what language fails to specify: blue with undertones of green where depth increases, purple where angle permits, gold where sun strikes directly, the color not stable but processual, each wave face presenting different surface, different reflection, different participation in light's interaction with matter.

The crowd has materialized as if from nowhere, though from everywhere actually—apartments releasing their inhabitants as heat decreases, shops closing or opening depending on commercial logic, the city's population redistributing itself from interior to exterior, from private to public, the circulation that evening enables, requires, and celebrates. Families walk in formations that declare relationships—parents flanking children, grandparents following slowly, the generations synchronized temporarily despite different velocities, different destinations, different relationships to time's passage.

A young couple passes, her hand touching his arm briefly, the contact minimal but significant, the public display of affection that Alexandria permits within strict parameters, the negotiation between desire and propriety that every culture manages differently, that here requires subtlety, coding, the messages transmitted through gesture rather than declaration. They walk close but not too close, together but maintaining plausible deniability, the relationship existing in liminal space between the sanctioned and the forbidden, the zone where most life actually occurs.

The evening promenade—la passeggiata in Italian, el paseo in Spanish, but no specific Arabic term, the practice transcending linguistic boundaries, occurring wherever humans concentrate along coasts, the sea drawing consciousness toward itself as gravity draws mass, or as mass creates gravity, the causation ambiguous, bidirectional. Every Mediterranean city performs this ritual, has performed it for centuries, will continue until cities cease or seas dry or humans evolve beyond the need for collective presence, for the confirmation that others exist, that solitude is chosen rather than imposed, that the day ends with witness, with participation in something larger than individual consciousness but smaller than abstract humanity.

Vendors have established positions along the wall—corn grilled over charcoal, the smoke carrying caramelized sweetness; nuts measured in paper cones, salt crystallizing on warm surfaces; tea in glasses that burn fingers, requiring careful handling, the minor risk that makes consumption intentional rather than automatic. The economics of it: small amounts, small prices, the accumulation that might enable survival but not prosperity, the informal sector that employs thousands, that exists outside taxation, regulation, the official economy that pretends to encompass all exchange but captures only what chooses visibility.

Music arrives—an oud player, perhaps sixty, the instrument worn but maintained, the wood polished by decades of handling. He plays without amplification, the sound barely audible above conversation, traffic, the sea's constant presence, but audible enough for those who choose to listen, who pause in their walking, who recognize in the melody something older than the city. A few coins accumulate in the case, enough for tea, for bread, for another evening's performance, the cycle continuing.

Children run between walkers, their energy

inexhaustible, apparently, though exhaustion will come, suddenly, completely, the collapse that parents anticipate, prepare for, the carrying home of sleeping bodies that moments before were perpetual motion. They chase pigeons that barely flee, that have adapted to human density, that continue their scavenging undisturbed by anything short of direct contact. The birds, too, are part of the evening's ecology, their presence neither welcomed nor prevented, simply accepted as a consequence of human concentration, of food dropped, discarded, the waste that becomes a resource in a different metabolic cycle.

"The sea is generous today."

The voice is familiar—the fisherman from dawn, now returning or still here or here again, the temporal sequence uncertain. He carries no fish, no equipment, the evidence of his profession absent, but the weathering remains, the skin that declares decades of solar exposure, salt accumulation, the body marked by its environment, shaped by repetitive action, the shoulders that have pulled nets, the hands that have gutted fish, the knowledge embodied rather than abstracted.

"The city requires witnessing."

The phrase emerges without planning, the echo of afternoon's old man, the wisdom borrowed, transmitted, modified in transmission. The fisherman nods, understanding or seeming to, the acceptance that doesn't require elaboration.

"Tomorrow I fish before dawn. Same time, same place. The sea doesn't wait, but it doesn't hurry."

He moves on, the interaction complete, its brevity sufficient, the exchange of recognition that doesn't become obligation, that acknowledges shared presence without demanding continued engagement. This too is urban knowledge—when to engage, when to release, the calibration of social distance that makes density bearable.

The sea doesn't wait, but it doesn't hurry. The temporal paradox that contains truth: processes proceed at their own rates, neither accelerated by desire nor delayed by reluctance. The tide rises and falls according to lunar gravity, not human need. Fish migrate following temperature gradients, food sources, and reproductive imperatives that consciousness can map but not modify. The fisherman knows this, works within it rather than against it, the submission to patterns larger than the individual will that makes his profession possible, that makes any engagement with nature more than extraction, that becomes participation, collaboration, the mutual modification that doesn't require mutual recognition.

The sun has descended to perhaps twenty degrees above the horizon, the angle that photographers pursue, that makes surfaces gold, that transforms the ordinary through illumination that won't last, that is precious because it is temporary.

The crowd has thickened, the Corniche now dense with bodies, the flow resembling fluid dynamics, laminar where space permits, turbulent at obstacles, eddies forming behind vendors, around musicians, the physics of crowds that mirrors the physics of fluids, same equations, different scales.

A young girl takes a selfie with sunset behind her, the image reviewed, deleted, retaken, the iteration continuing until satisfaction or exhaustion, the documentation that precedes experience, that might replace experience, the photograph more real than the moment it claims to preserve. Her friend watches, waits, and offers to take a photo that includes both—the paradox of staged authenticity that social media demands, rewards, and normalizes.

Beyond them, the sun touches a cloud layer that hasn't been visible until now, the moisture invisible until light reveals it, transforms it, and makes it spectacular, temporarily. The colours proliferate—orange, pink, purple, the spectrum's warm end dominating while blue retreats, persists only in zenith, the sky becomes a gradient, transition made visible. The crowd notices, some stopping to observe, others continuing their walk, the sunset ordinary through repetition, through reliability, the spectacle that happens daily therefore barely happens, consciousness habituating to wonder, requiring novelty that nature doesn't provide, proceeding through cycles that vary within patterns, that repeat without exact repetition.

Beauty is consciousness's category, not

nature's. The sunset proceeds according to physics—Rayleigh scattering, atmospheric refraction, and the geometry of celestial mechanics. The colours exist in perception, wavelengths interpreted by neural processing that evolved for different purposes, that find beauty where utility once existed, the aesthetic judgment that might be an evolutionary spandrel, an accidental consequence of pattern recognition necessary for survival. But knowing the physics doesn't diminish the experience, might enhance it—*understanding process while participating in it*, the double consciousness that science enables, that poetry preceded, that philosophy attempts to reconcile.

He finds a space at the wall, claims it through presence, the informal property rights that govern public space, which last only while occupied, and that dissolve with departure. The stone is warm still from day's accumulation, the thermal mass releasing slowly what it absorbed quickly, the hysteresis that makes coastal climates moderate, that makes the Mediterranean's shores habitable, that will make them uninhabitable when temperatures exceed what the stone can buffer, what bodies can endure.

An old man stands nearby, perhaps the same from the afternoon's fountain, perhaps different, the elderly becoming a category rather than individuals in consciousness that doesn't attend carefully, that generalizes from limited samples, that sees pattern where there might be randomness. He watches the sunset with attention that suggests practice, routine, the daily observation that might be meditation, might be a simple occupation of time that must be occupied somehow, that stretches when productivity ceases, when purpose becomes survival rather than accomplishment.

"Every evening?" Hakim asks the question that is also acknowledgment, invitation, and the opening of potential exchange.

"When possible. Which is usually. At my age, everything is usually or never."

The response carries humour without joke, the acceptance of the constraint that age imposes, that consciousness recognizes but the body experiences, the difference between knowing and being that philosophy articulates but life demonstrates.

"You're not from here," the man continues. "I thought I would find something," Hakim offers, the admission incomplete but sufficient.

"You came to discover you can't arrive at what was only textual, but you found what everyone finds—difference. But difference from what?

The man's Arabic is formal, educated, the syntax of someone who reads, who thinks in structured ways, who might have been a teacher, scholar, one of Alexandria's intellectuals who stayed when others left, who maintained civilization's conversation in place while others carried it elsewhere.

"You taught," Hakim suggests, reading the signs, the

posture, the particular attention to language's precision.

"Philosophy. At the University. Forty years. Retired now, which means I do the same thing without office, without students, without purpose except purpose itself. I read, I think, I watch sunset, I sleep, I wake, I continue. Same activity, different audience. Or no audience, which might be more honest. Philosophy performed for witnesses becomes performance, loses something essential. Philosophy without an audience might be madness, but it might be purity. The distinction is unclear and might be meaningless. The examined life, which Socrates said was the only life worth living, though he didn't live long enough to test the hypothesis fully."

Philosophy without an audience might be madness, but it might be purity. This is the question that haunts all thinking that thinks about thinking—is consciousness examining itself productive or recursive, does it generate insight or infinite regress, does it approach truth or create elaborate fictions that console but don't correspond. The examined life might be worth living, but is examining the examined life worth doing, and examining that examination, the recursion that philosophy enables, suffers, might be its glory or might be its failure.

They stand together, watching the sun approach the horizon, the disc now visible without pain, the intensity diminished enough that looking is possible, that the eye can perceive the sphere that is always there but usually unbearable, the source that makes sight possible but blinds when observed directly, the paradox of illumination that reveals everything except itself.

"The sea does not care," the philosopher says, "which is why it's perfect. Every wave is new water arranged in an ancient pattern. Identity without substance, form without matter, or rather form constantly acquiring new matter, discarding it, acquiring again. This is what we are too—patterns temporarily organized, mistaking ourselves for permanent, discovering impermanence, struggling to accept what was always obvious."

Every wave is new water arranged in an ancient pattern. This is *process philosophy* articulated simply, precisely, the wisdom that doesn't require technical terminology, that emerges from observation, from attention sustained over decades, from the thinking that walking enables, that sitting prevents, that makes philosophy peripatetic necessarily, not arbitrarily. The pattern persists while matter transforms—this is identity, this is consciousness, this is everything that seems stable but is actually dynamic equilibrium, the balance that requires constant adjustment, constant energy, constant participation.

The sun touches the horizon now, the moment that is not moment but duration, the disc's lower edge meeting the line that is not line but curve, the Earth's rotation made visible or rather the effect of rotation, the relative motion that consciousness experiences as sunset, though nothing sets, nothing rises, the language preserving pre-Copernican cosmology, the phenomenology that persists despite knowledge, that remains true experientially while false astronomically.

The crowd has quieted, not silent but subdued, the collective attention that sunset commands, that makes strangers a temporary community, witnessing together what each could witness alone but chooses not to, the gathering that makes an event from occurrence, that transforms daily process into ritual, into the repetition that creates culture, that distinguishes human consciousness from mere awareness.

Musicians have multiplied—the oud player joined by a tabla drummer, the rhythm establishing itself, finding the tempo that walking creates, that bodies recognize, that makes movement music and music movement. Some children dance, their movements unselfconscious, uncalculated, the response that precedes thought, that thought later inhibits, that adulthood mostly eliminates except in moments when consciousness relaxes its control, permits body its knowledge, its own intelligence that modernism calls primitive but is actually primary, foundational, the wisdom of muscle and bone that preceded language, that will outlast it.

The sun is half-disappeared now, the process accelerating apparently, though the rate is constant, the perception shifting as reference points change, as the disc's visible portion diminishes, as consciousness attends more carefully, knowing conclusion approaches. The colors have deepened—orange becoming red, purple darkening toward violet, the blue overhead persisting but different blue, darker, preparing for night's arrival that is not arrival but continuation, the spectrum shifting beyond visible, the infrared that bodies feel as warmth, the ultraviolet that damages but doesn't announce itself, the electromagnetic radiation that consciousness samples narrowly, interprets partially, mistakes for complete.

Sunset is not an event but a process, not a conclusion but a transition. The sun continues its fusion, the Earth continues its rotation, the only ending is in consciousness that divides continuous process into discrete moments, that creates boundaries where none exist, that makes meaning from patterns that proceed without meaning, that don't require meaning, that exist before meaning and will exist after.

We are sunset's witnesses, not its purpose. It

would proceed without us, has proceeded for billions of years without consciousness, will proceed after consciousness ceases, the universe continuing its expansion, its transformation toward heat death that is not death but a different configuration, different process, the possibility we can't imagine because imagination requires negentropy that won't exist, can't exist, in a universe at thermal equilibrium.

The philosopher has been quiet, watching, perhaps thinking or perhaps not, the attention that doesn't require thought, that might be thought's absence, the awareness without analysis that meditation seeks, that walking sometimes enables, that sunset might facilitate through beauty that overwhelms cognitive processing, that forces consciousness to receive rather than interpret, to participate rather than evaluate.

"You wrote today," he observes, noting something—ink stains perhaps, or the particular fatigue that sustained writing produces, or simply the deduction from Hakim's manner, the way consciousness shaped by writing carries itself, announces itself.

"Notes. Observations. Trying to understand something."

"Understanding is overvalued. Participating is undervalued. The sea doesn't understand itself, but continues. The sun doesn't understand fusion, but fuses.

Understanding is consciousness's compensation for not being able to simply *be*, to continue without question, to process without purpose."

The statement could be nihilistic, but it isn't; it carries acceptance rather than resignation, the wisdom that comes from thinking through to thought's limits, discovering what lies beyond, which is not nothing but something else, something that doesn't require articulation, that exists without language, that language points toward but can't contain.

The sun's final edge disappears, the moment marked by some with photographs, by others with silence, by children with indifference, their games continuing, their energy not yet depleted. The sky continues its chromatic display, the colors persisting after their source has passed below horizon, the atmosphere itself luminous, scattering light that arrives indirectly, the sunset that continues after sunset, the process that doesn't conclude but transforms, continues elsewhere, the terminator sweeping westward, bringing night here, day there, the planet's rotation ensuring that every sunset is also sunrise, every ending also beginning, the cycle that is not cycle but spiral, repetition with variation, pattern with progress or at least change, which might be progress, might be decay, might be simply difference without evaluation.

"Walk with me," the philosopher suggests, beginning to move before response, assuming acceptance, the invitation that is barely an invitation, more observation that walking will occur, that consciousness at rest tends toward rest, while consciousness in motion tends toward motion, the inertia that applies to thought as to matter.

They walk eastward now, the sun behind them. The

crowd has begun to thin slightly, families with young children departing, the demographic shifting toward adolescents, young adults, those whose evening extends beyond sunset, whose social life begins when families' end.

"You practice medicine," the philosopher observes, states, and knows somehow.

"Practiced. Blood," Hakim replied.

"The most philosophical of substances. Liquid but structured, identical but unique, constantly renewed but recognizably continuous. Blood is a process made visible, made vital. Without circulation, blood is just fluid. Without blood, circulation is just plumbing."

The observation is accurate, insightful, the connection between medical and philosophical that Hakim has thought but not articulated, which requires external confirmation, the recognition that thinking alone doesn't provide, that makes conversation necessary despite thought's tendency toward solitude.

They continue walking, the rhythm established, the pace that enables conversation without breathlessness, that synchronizes their movements, that creates temporary unity from separate consciousnesses, the shared ambulation that might be communication's oldest form, preceding language, the walking together that establishes trust, that enables exchange, that makes strangers into temporary companions.

The stars have begun to appear, not suddenly but gradually, the brightest first—Venus probably, though planets don't twinkle, the steady light that distinguishes them from stars whose light atmospheric turbulence disturbs, makes dance, the scintillation that poetry celebrates but astronomy corrects for, the distortion that must be subtracted to see clearly what distance and time have brought to visibility.

"Alexandria had astronomers," the philosopher notes, following Hakim's gaze upward. "Mapped the stars, calculated orbits, and understood celestial mechanics centuries before telescopes. The Library wasn't just a storage but a laboratory, observatory, the place where knowledge was produced, not just preserved. We forget that, imagine it as an archive when it was actually a workshop, the place where understanding was manufactured, processed, refined."

"And lost," Hakim adds, the obvious conclusion.

"Lost implies it existed stably, could be preserved. But knowledge is a process, not a product. It exists only in transmission, in teaching, in the movement from mind to mind. The Library burned, yes, but the librarians dispersed, carried what they remembered, taught elsewhere, the diaspora that preserved through transformation what storage couldn't maintain unchanged."

Knowledge is a process, not a product. This reformulation challenges everything academic culture assumes: the publications that fix thought in text, the libraries that store publications, the citations that create genealogies of ideas as if ideas were objects rather than events, things rather than happenings. But every reading is a new reading, every understanding is a new understanding, the text might be stable, but interpretation isn't, can't be, the meaning emerging from interaction between consciousness and marks on page, the participation that makes dead letters living thought, temporarily, until attention moves elsewhere.

The Corniche continues, seems infinite though finite obviously, Alexandria's edge being defined, limited, where Mediterranean meets land, the boundaries that seem permanent but are negotiated constantly, the sea claiming land through erosion, storms, the land claiming sea through sedimentation, construction, the interface that is not line but zone, area of contest, exchange, the liminal space where categories blur.

"You visit but don't stay," the philosopher observes, predicts, knows.

"Probably not. The visit was necessary but not sustainable. I came to..." Hakim pauses, the purpose suddenly unclear, inarticulate, the motivation that seemed obvious now mysterious, the forces that produced the visit too complex to name simply.

"You came to discover you can't stay. Everyone does. The emigrants, especially the successful ones, particularly. They achieve elsewhere what here was impossible, then discover achievement doesn't satisfy, that success is local, contextual, that what matters there doesn't matter here, that here doesn't exist anyway, has become there while you were away, the place transformed by your absence as much as by time's passage."

The diagnosis is accurate, uncomfortable, the truth that Hakim has been discovering all day made explicit, external, and undeniable. The philosopher continues:

"But the attempt matters. The walking, the witnessing, the writing you did today. Not because it discovers anything but because it processes, transforms, enables tomorrow's difference. You'll leave Alexandria but Alexandria won't leave you, will continue in memory that will continue lying, creating, making meaning from patterns that exceed meaning. This is participation—not presence but process, not being here but having been here, the past that enables future, the accumulation that makes consciousness more than immediate awareness."

They've reached a pause, a place where the philosopher apparently intends to stop, to turn, to continue alone or elsewhere. The interaction is concluding, has reached its natural term, the exchange is complete, though completion is always arbitrary, provisional, the conversation could continue, but won't, the timing that social intelligence recognizes, respects.

"Tomorrow morning," the philosopher says, "same sun, same sea, different consciousness observing. The repetition that is never repetition, the pattern that persists through variation, the process that includes us temporarily. Walk early, before the heat. Think less, observe more. Write if you must, but remember writing is also a process, also a transformation, the meaning you create is not discovered but made, manufactured, the product that is actually production, the making that never completes."

He walks away without farewell, the departure that doesn't require ceremony, the urban anonymity that permits encounter without obligation, exchange without commitment, the freedom that density enables, that makes cities laboratories for consciousness, for the experiments in living that suburbs prevent, that villages prohibit, that only the metropolitan allows, demands, and makes possible.

Hakim stands alone now, the evening continuing around him, through him, the crowd that has thinned but not disappeared, the energy that has shifted from familial to social, from display to encounter, the night beginning its different processes, its different possibilities.

The walk back is quick, directed, the body knowing the route now, the cognitive map established, the efficiency that familiarity enables. The streets are different at night—lit differently, populated differently, the same coordinates containing a different city, the nocturnal Alexandria that coexists with diurnal, that occupies the same space but different time, the temporal zoning that makes multiple cities possible in a single location.

The apartment building is quiet, the stairs dark, the ascent careful, touch supplementing vision, the proprioceptive knowledge that bodies develop, which makes navigation possible without sight, the backup systems that consciousness doesn't acknowledge until needed. The door opens to a space that is beginning to become familiar, the repetition that makes strange into known, that transforms space into place through duration, through return, through the accumulation of moments that memory will reconstruct, falsify, and make meaningful.

Today is complete but not concluded, will continue in memory, in dream, in tomorrow's difference that today enables. The Mediterranean continues its circulation, its process, its indifference that is not hostility but freedom, the freedom from meaning that enables meaning, that makes consciousness possible, necessary, temporary, grateful.

The pen stops, the notebook closes, and evening yields to night.

NIGHT

Eight-thirty and darkness has begun its establishment, not arrival but intensification, the photons decreasing exponentially, the electromagnetic radiation shifting beyond visible spectrum, the infrared that bodies emit, detect through thermal receptors, the heat signatures that make us visible to different sensors, the night vision that technology enables, that evolution provided to nocturnal predators but not to primates whose ancestors chose daylight, traded night vision for color discrimination, the evolutionary bargain that makes darkness foreign to consciousness that depends on light for more than sight, for the metaphors that structure thought itself—enlightenment, illumination, clarity, the cognitive dependence on optical experience.

The Corniche has transformed, demographically, energetically, the families replaced by different congregations—young men in groups whose solidarity is performed through proximity, volume, the occupation of space that asserts presence, claims territory, establishes identity through collective embodiment. Young women are also in groups, but differently configured; the protection that numbers provide, the surveillance that continues despite darkness, perhaps intensified by it.

Hakim walks among them but not of them, the distance that age creates, the anthropological position that observes while participating minimally, enough to avoid suspicion, not enough to be included. The sea is audible but barely visible, its presence announced through sound—waves continuous but irregular, the arhythmic rhythm that consciousness tries to pattern, fails, tries again, the repetition without exact repetition that defines natural processes, that distinguishes them from mechanical reproduction, from the industrial consistency that modernity mistakes for perfection.

The stars have achieved full visibility, as full as light pollution permits, the astronomical loss that urbanization requires, accepts, and forgets to mourn. Orion rises in the east, the constellation that ancient Egyptians associated with Osiris, that Greeks saw as hunter, that astronomy recognizes as asterism, chance alignment from Earth's perspective, the stars actually at different distances, unrelated except through projection, the meaning consciousness creates from random distribution, the patterns that exist only in perception, from particular position, at particular time, the cosmic accident of viewpoint that makes meaning possible, necessary, false.

Night is not day's absence but a different presence, not negation but alternative, the processes that darkness enables, requires—sleep, dreams, the nocturnal ecology, the crimes and consolations that light inhibits. Consciousness evolved for daylight, struggles with darkness, fears it appropriately, the vulnerability that unconsciousness creates, that sleep demands, the daily rehearsal of death that rest requires, that bodies insist upon despite the mind's resistance. We are diurnal temporarily, nocturnally, the third of life spent unconscious, the processes continuing without awareness—circulation, respiration, digestion, the autonomic functions that preceded consciousness, that enable it, that will outlast it briefly when brain ceases but body continues, the minutes or hours when blood still circulates through dead tissue, when cells continue metabolizing until oxygen depletes, when death proceeds gradually, systematically, the process that medicine can now reverse partially, temporarily, the boundary become zone, area rather than line.

A group of teenagers has assembled around someone's phone, watching a video that produces collective laughter, the shared screen that creates temporary community, the mediation that brings together while keeping apart, each viewing from a slightly different angle, receiving a different image, the parallax that makes every experience unique despite sharing the source. They don't notice Hakim passing, their attention absorbed, captured, the attention economy that extracts value from consciousness, that monetizes awareness, that makes a product from what was process, a commodity from what was capacity.

The notebook remains in the apartment but memory records, processes, begins the forgetting that is also transformation, the selective retention that creates narrative from experience, meaning from randomness, the story consciousness tells itself about what happened, which is never what happened but what needed to happen for consciousness to continue, to maintain coherence that might be illusion but is necessary illusion, functional fiction, the lie that enables truth or at least continuation.

An old woman sits alone on a bench, feeding cats that emerge from shadows, approach cautiously, accept food while maintaining distance, the calibrated trust that street animals develop, that enables survival without domestication. She speaks to them, the monologue that is also a dialogue, the cats responding through presence if not language, the interspecies communication that doesn't require a shared code, that operates through gesture, positioning, the embodied knowledge that preceded language, that remains when language fails.

"They remember," she says, noticing Hakim noticing, including him involuntarily in her practice. "Each night, same time, same place. They know I'll come. I know they'll come. This is all a relationship requires—reliable presence, mutual recognition, the pattern that continues until it doesn't."

Until it doesn't. The phrase that acknowledges termination without specifying it, that recognizes ending as possibility, probability, certainty eventually, but not yet, not tonight, the continuation that is always temporary but is temporary for now, the now that is all consciousness actually has despite memory's claim on past, anticipation's claim on future, the present that is present only briefly, immediately becoming past, the moment that exists only in passing, that cannot be held, examined, possessed, only experienced in its vanishing, its transformation into memory that is already interpretation, already fiction, already lost.

The darkness has deepened, the transition complete enough that eyes have adapted, pupils dilated, rhodopsin regenerated, the chemistry of vision adjusted for scotopic conditions though scotopic is relative, the city never achieving true darkness, the light pollution that makes astronomy impossible, that erases stars, that replaces cosmos with streetlights, the trade that urbanization requires, the loss that most don't recognize as loss, having never known true darkness, the darkness that reveals the Milky Way, the galaxy's edge-on view, the billions of stars that surround us, that we're part of, that consciousness emerged from, temporarily, accidentally, magnificently, meaninglessly, meaningfully.

He continues walking, eastward again, the circuit approaching completion though completion is arbitrary, the starting point being chosen not given, the boundary that consciousness creates then treats as real, as significant, the meaning-making that can't be stopped, that might be consciousness's essence if consciousness has essence, which process philosophy denies, insisting on process not essence, becoming not being, the verbal preference that might be mere preference or might be recognition of something fundamental, something that substance metaphysics misses, mistakes, the error that millennia of philosophy have sustained, that process thought attempts to correct, perhaps overcorrects, the pendulum swinging from substance to process, missing the middle that might not exist, the balance that might be impossible.

A man approaches, drunk or tired or both, his gait irregular, compensating, the body maintaining balance despite impairment, the proprioceptive intelligence that operates below awareness, that keeps us upright, oriented, the vestibular system that evolved from fish's lateral line, the gravity sensors that work continuously, unconsciously, the background processing that consciousness depends on but doesn't acknowledge, like the heart's beating, like the liver's filtration, like the kidneys' regulation, the processes that continue whether attended or not, that attention might disrupt, that function best when forgotten.

"Doctor," the man says, the identification unclear—does he recognize Hakim specifically or identify him as type, the class markers that persist despite attempted erasure, the habitus that Bourdieu described, the embodied cultural capital that announces itself through posture, gesture, the subtle signals that locate individuals socially, economically, and educationally.

"I'm not practicing," Hakim responds, the clarification that is also a deflection, the boundary setting that urban interaction requires.

"No one is practicing," the man responds, the statement cryptic, philosophical perhaps or perhaps just drunk wisdom, the profundity that intoxication sometimes enables, sometimes mimics, the altered consciousness that might access different truths or might just be altered, the consciousness that is always already altered anyway, by culture, by language, by the particular configuration of neurotransmitters, hormones, the chemistry that makes experience possible, that makes experience particular, that ensures no two consciousnesses experience identically, the solipsism that empathy attempts to bridge but can't, not fully, the gap that makes individuals individual, alone, together in aloneness.

The man continues past, the encounter brief, ambiguous, already becoming an anecdote, a story, the transformation of experience into narrative that consciousness performs continuously, compulsively, the story-making that might be adaptation, might be pathology, might be simply what this configuration of matter does under these conditions, the emergence that complexity enables, requires, the whole exceeding the sum of parts, consciousness exceeding neurons, meaning exceeding information, the excess that is everything or nothing depending on perspective, depending on what matters, what can matter, what we make matter.

The sea at night is a different sea, not visually but auditorily, the sound carrying further in cooler air, the density differential that makes sound waves propagate differently, the physics that consciousness experiences as atmosphere, as mood, as the night's particular quality that is not mystical but physical, measurable, the decibels and frequencies that instruments detect, that consciousness interprets, that become experience, that become memory, that become the story of walking by the sea at night, the story that is not false but is not true either, is something else, something between or beyond truth and falsity, the third category that experience occupies, that consciousness creates, inhabits, shares through language that translates experience into communicable form, losing everything essential, preserving everything essential, the paradox that communication is, that consciousness accepts, must accept to not be alone, to maintain the fiction of shared experience, shared meaning, shared world.

The apartment building approaches, or he approaches it, the question of who moves toward whom being relative, depending on reference frame, the physics that Einstein clarified but that consciousness still struggles with, the intuition that makes us geocentric, anthropocentric, egocentric, the center that is nowhere but seems to be wherever consciousness is, the privileged position that is not privilege but prison, the inability to escape our own perspective, to see from nowhere, to achieve the view that objectivity claims but can't deliver, the situated knowledge that is all knowledge despite pretensions otherwise.

But he doesn't enter, not yet, the night not yet exhausted, the body tired but consciousness alert, the dissociation that evening creates, that makes sleep difficult despite fatigue, the circadian disruption that modern life enables, electricity defeating darkness, screens defeating sleep, the evolutionary mismatch that makes insomnia epidemic, the inability to rest that capitalism produces, exploits, the twenty-four hour economy that never sleeps, that makes sleep seem like failure, weakness, the missing of opportunity, the fear of missing out that keeps consciousness vigilant, exhausted, unable to stop.

At the sea wall again, different position than morning, than afternoon, than evening, the same sea but different angle, different sound, the waves approaching from darkness, visible only at the last moment when streetlight catches foam, the white briefly brilliant then gone, swallowed by darkness that is not absence but presence of a different kind, the darkness that has mass, weight, the psychological experience of darkness as substance, as a thing rather than nothing, the phenomenology that contradicts physics but persists, the experience that is real regardless of accuracy, that makes darkness frightening, comforting, both, neither, depending on context, condition, the state of consciousness that encounters it.

I came here seeking something, and found something else, the substitution that is not failure but education, the learning that occurs through disappointment, through the discovery that what we seek doesn't exist, never existed except in imagination that projected onto world what world doesn't contain, can't contain, the meaning that must be made not found, the purpose that must be created not discovered, the hard wisdom that consciousness achieves or doesn't, that makes adulthood possible or impossible, that distinguishes maturity from mere aging, the acceptance that the universe doesn't care, can't care, that care is consciousness's addition, projection, gift to itself, the strange loop of meaning-making in meaningless cosmos, the defiance that is also submission, the rebellion that is also acceptance.

A couple passes, elderly, walking slowly, her hand through his arm, the support that is mutual, the balance achieved together that neither could maintain alone, the interdependence that age makes visible, that youth disguises, the fiction of independence that bodies maintain temporarily then surrender, the vulnerability that is a human condition despite technological mediation, despite medical intervention, despite the longevity that modernity provides some, denies others, the inequality that makes some bodies worth preserving, others disposable, the economics of life that capitalism calculates, that consciousness rejects but participates in, the complicity that contemporary existence requires.

They nod, the acknowledgment that night walkers exchange, the recognition of shared nocturnality, the choice to be out when convention suggests inside, the mild rebellion that walking at night represents, the claim to public space when public has retired, when space becomes different, charged with different possibilities, different dangers, the night that enables and threatens, that consciousness navigates carefully, alertly, the vigilance that darkness demands, that exhausts, that makes tomorrow's rest necessary, inevitable.

"The sea never sleeps," the old man says in passing, the observation offered without expecting response, the gift of recognition, of shared attention to what continues while consciousness pauses, the processes that don't require witness but receive it, temporarily, gratefully perhaps, though gratitude implies consciousness that the sea lacks, the anthropomorphism that language enables, requires, the metaphor that is an error but a necessary error, a functional mistake, the projection that makes world speakable, even if falsely.

Stars reflect on water when waves permit, the light that left those stars years, centuries, millennia ago arriving now, hitting retina, creating the experience of a star that might no longer exist, that probably has changed, moved, the light carrying information about a past that masquerades as a present, the temporal confusion that astronomy accepts, works with, the knowledge that what we see is what was, that present is inaccessible, that universe is experienced historically, through delay, the gap between the event and the perception that increases with distance, that makes cosmos archaeological, the past visible, the present invisible, and the future unknowable.

Death is certain but not tonight, probably, the calculation that consciousness makes continuously, unconsciously, the risk assessment that keeps us functional despite mortality's certainty, the denial that is not denial but postponement, the reasonable assumption that patterns will continue until they don't, that tomorrow will arrive for me though not for everyone, the statistics that make individual death unlikely while making collective death certain, the mathematics that consciousness can't fully grasp, that makes us act as if immortal while knowing we're mortal, the cognitive dissonance that enables planning, hoping, the future orientation that makes the present bearable, meaningful, despite the future's certainty of ending, of consciousness ceasing, of the processes that are me dispersing, transforming, continuing differently, without me, the me that is a pattern not a substance, that is a temporary coordination of processes that preceded me, that continue through me, that will continue after, the after that I won't experience, that is unimaginable despite imagination's efforts, the blank that death is for consciousness that can imagine everything except its own absence.

Time to return, to climb stairs one more time today, the repetition that makes routine, that makes place from space, that creates belonging through duration, even if belonging is fiction, projection, the meaning assigned rather than discovered. The door opens to darkness that familiarity makes navigable, the muscle memory that bodies develop, that makes motion automatic, efficient, the unconscious competence that frees consciousness for other tasks or for no task, for the rest that approaches, that demands submission, that consciousness resists until resistance fails, until exhaustion wins, until sleep arrives, departs, and arrives again, the cycle within cycle, the rhythm that bodies insist upon, that culture disrupts, that modernity makes difficult, that night enables despite electricity, despite screens, despite the attempt to make night into day, to eliminate darkness, to maintain consciousness continuously, the impossible project that fails nightly, that must fail for sanity, for health, for the processes that sleep enables, the memory consolidation, the cellular repair, the dreams that process what consciousness can't, that make sense from nonsense or nonsense from sense, the distinction unclear, perhaps meaningless.

The notebook opens one final time, the day demanding a conclusion, though conclusion is arbitrary, the boundaries consciousness create then treat as real.

The pen moves across paper, the marks that encode meaning, that will survive the consciousness that made them, briefly, the material trace that writing is, the death defying that is also death acknowledging, the attempt to persist through signs that outlast bodies, that communicate across time, that make past present for future consciousness that reads, interprets, misunderstands necessarily, the translation that reading is, that communication requires, that ensures meaning changes even when words remain stable, the process that writing initiates but doesn't control, can't control, the release that publication is, the death that authorship requires, the meaning leaving maker, becoming other, becoming public, becoming process rather than product.

Mediterranean night. The sea continues its

circulation invisible, but continuing, the process that doesn't pause for darkness, that doesn't require light, that operates through forces that preceded consciousness, that will outlast it. The day is complete—not concluded but complete in its incompletion, its partial view, its limited understanding, its temporary participation in processes that exceed comprehension but include it, permit it, enable the meaning-making that might be error, might be gift, might be simply what happens when matter organizes at this level of complexity, for this duration, under these conditions. Tomorrow there will be another dawn, another day, another opportunity to participate, to witness, to make meaning from patterns that need no meaning, that continue regardless, that include consciousness temporarily in their continuation, their process, their indifference that is not cruelty but freedom, the freedom that makes meaning possible because meaning is not given, required, the freedom that makes consciousness tragic and magnificent, temporary and necessary, impossible and actual. The sea doesn't remember today. I will remember for both of us, inaccurately, creatively, the memory that is not preservation but transformation, that makes past present, that enables future, that continues the process of processing, of participating, of being temporarily what processes provisionally produce, the pattern that coheres briefly then disperses, that calls itself *I*, that writes these words, that sleeps, dreams, wakes, continues until it doesn't, until the pattern dissolves, the processes continue differently, the sea remains.

The pen stops, final, sufficient. The notebook closes. The lamp extinguishes. Darkness returns, welcomed now, necessary, the darkness that is not ending but transition, the daily rehearsal for final darkness that will come, not tonight, probably not tomorrow, eventually certainly, the certainty that makes each day significant or insignificant, both simultaneously, the paradox that consciousness is, embodies, can't resolve, doesn't need to resolve, the tension that generates meaning, movement, the process that is life, that is consciousness, that is this day, complete.

Sleep approaches, consciousness beginning its dissolution, its temporary cessation, the processes continuing but awareness withdrawing, the mysterious transition from conscious to unconscious, the boundary that neuroscience maps but doesn't understand, the hard problem's nightly demonstration, the consciousness that somehow emerges from matter returning to matter, temporarily, reversibly, until the irreversible return, the final dissolution, but not tonight, tonight is sleep not death, process not conclusion, the continuation that tomorrow assumes, requires, enables.

The Mediterranean continues. Alexandria sleeps, mostly, the city's metabolism slowing but not stopping, the night shift workers, the insomniacs, the criminals, the lonely, maintaining minimal consciousness, keeping the city barely alive, ready for tomorrow's reanimation. Somewhere, dawn is breaking. Here darkness deepens.

The cycle continues. The process processes. The pattern persists, temporarily, sufficiently, necessarily, actually. This is enough.

9 781999 065645